www.FlowerpotPress.com
CHC-0909-0465
ISBN: 978-1-4867-1583-1
Made in China/Fabriqué en Chine

# Moo, Moo, Moo, Chew, Chew, Chew

## Sounds from the Farm

# Did you hear that?

I hear moo, moo, moo and chew, chew, chew

with a swish,
swish,
swish going
swat, swat,
swat!

It's a cow mooing and chewing as his tail swishes and swats!

I hear oink, oink, oink and snort, snort, snort!

# Wallow, wallow, wallow and squeal, squeal, squeal!

It's the pigs squealing and snorting in the mud!

I hear honk, honk, honk! They're moving with a waddle, waddle, waddle

**and ruffle,
ruffle, ruffle
and flap,
flap, flap!**

It's a gaggle of geese honking and waddling as they wander around!

I hear neigh, neigh, neigh, neigh and trot, trot, trot!

# Whinny, whinny, whinny going clippity-clop, clippity-clop!

It's a trotting horse
going clippity-clop,
clop, clop!

I hear **cluck, cluck, cluck, cluck** and peck, peck, peck!

# Scratch, scratch, scratch and a cock-a-doodle-doo!

It's the chickens and the rooster
pecking and clucking all about!

I hear hee-haw, hee-haw!
It's moving slow with a shuffle, shuffle, shuffle

and a scuffle,
scuffle, scuffle
and a dawdle,
dawdle,
dawdle!

It's a dawdling
donkey shuffling
and scuffling!

I hear slurp, slurp, slurp and gulp, gulp, gulp

**with all sorts of splish, splish, splish and splash, splash, splash!**

It's all the farm animals slurping
and gulping at the water trough!

# Wait...
# Did you hear that?